YOU GO FIRST

written by Ariel Bernstein ❀ illustrated by Marc Rosenthal

A Paula Wiseman Book · Simon & Schuster Books for Young Readers
New York London Toronto Sydney New Delhi

SIMON & SCHUSTER BOOKS FOR YOUNG READERS
An imprint of Simon & Schuster Children's Publishing Division
1230 Avenue of the Americas, New York, New York 10020
Text © 2023 by Ariel Bernstein Books LLC
Illustration © 2023 by Marc Rosenthal
Book design by Lizzy Bromley © 2023 by Simon & Schuster, Inc.

SIMON & SCHUSTER BOOKS FOR YOUNG READERS
and related marks are trademarks of Simon & Schuster, Inc.
For information about special discounts for bulk purchases, please contact
Simon & Schuster Special Sales at 1-866-506-1949 or business@simonandschuster.com.
The Simon & Schuster Speakers Bureau can bring authors to your live event.
For more information or to book an event, contact the Simon & Schuster Speakers Bureau at
1-866-248-3049 or visit our website at www.simonspeakers.com.
The text for this book was set in Adobe Caslon.
The illustrations for this book were rendered in Prismacolor pencil and digital color.
Manufactured in China • 0223 SCP • First Edition
2 4 6 8 10 9 7 5 3 1
Library of Congress Cataloging-in-Publication Data
Names: Bernstein, Ariel, author. | Rosenthal, Marc, 1949– illustrator.
Title: You go first / Ariel Bernstein ; illustrated by Marc Rosenthal.
Description: First edition. | New York : Simon & Schuster Books for Young Readers, [2023] | "A
Paula Wiseman Book." | Audience: Ages 4–8. | Audience: Grades 2–3. | Summary: Cat learns
that being a good friend means trying new things and putting others first.
Identifiers: LCCN 2022028277 (print) | LCCN 2022028278 (ebook) |
ISBN 9781665911511 (hardcover) | ISBN 9781665911528 (ebook)
Subjects: CYAC: Cats—Fiction. | Ducks—Fiction. | Friendship—Fiction. |
LCGFT: Animal fiction. | Picture books.
Classification: LCC PZ7.1.B463 Yo 2023 (print) | LCC PZ7.1.B463 (ebook) | DDC [E]—dc23
LC record available at https://lccn.loc.gov/2022028277
LC ebook record available at https://lccn.loc.gov/2022028278

To Tara, a very good friend
—A. B.

To my fellow scaredy-cats
—M. R.

Cat and Duck,
two very good friends,
arrived at the playground.
They wanted to go on the slide.

But something was different.

The slide was bigger.

The slide was curvier.

Cat, a very good friend,
wanted to make sure Duck
had considered all options.

No, Cat. I want to go
on the slide first.

Cat and Duck got in line for the slide.

Soon, they were halfway to the top.

Cat, a very good friend, worried that Duck needed a snack.

Duck, are you hungry?

No.

Are you thirsty?

No.

Think of waterfalls, rain showers, and waves crashing. Are you thirsty now?

No. But I have to use the bathroom.

Now Cat and Duck were
ready for the slide.

The family of pigs behind them looked ready for the slide too.

Cat, a very good friend, worried that Duck wasn't being polite enough.

Cat, a very good friend,
worried for Duck's safety.

It would be *more* safe if you had goggles.
Here, three pairs should do it.

You need a helmet, too.
And a parachute.

Cat, a very good friend, worried that Duck didn't understand how scary a newer, bigger, and curvier slide could be.

Duck, I must warn you. If you go down that slide, you may fall! And scream! And cry!

I could fall?

Yes.

I could scream?
I could cry?

Yes. And yes!

Thank you for looking out for me, Cat. I do not want to go on the slide anymore. Even if I was looking forward to it.

Cat, a very good friend, worried that Duck was going to miss out on something she wanted. Cat suddenly felt very, very bad.

Duck, you should go on the slide. It won't be too scary.
Gulp! I will show you. I will go first.

You will?

Yes. Here I go.

You just needed to go first.

Duck was a very good friend.